Get to know the girls of

Dancing Queen

BY
THALIA KALKIPSAKIS

ILLUSTRATED BY
ASH OSWALD

SQUARE
FISH

FEIWEL AND FRIENDS
NEW YORK

SQUARE
FISH

An Imprint of Macmillan
175 Fifth Avenue
New York, NY 10010
mackids.com

Our books may be purchased in bulk for promotional, educational,
or business use. Please contact your local bookseller or the
Macmillan Corporate and Premium Sales Department
at (800) 221-7945 ext. 5442 or by e-mail at
MacmillanSpecialMarkets@macmillan.com.

Library of Congress Cataloging-in-Publication Data Available

ISBN 978-1-250-09815-3

First published in Australia by E2,
an imprint of Hardie Grant Egmont.
Illustration and design by Ash Oswald.

First published in the United States by Feiwel and Friends
First U.S. Edition: 2008
Square Fish Reissue Edition: 2016
Square Fish logo designed by Filomena Tuosto

1 3 5 7 9 10 8 6 4 2

AR: 3.9

CHAPTER ONE

~Rosie's~
DANCE ACADEMY

Charlie looked up at the sign and grinned. Here she was at last—at a real dance school. No more dancing in the cold church basement. No more boring ballet classes with old Miss Plum.

Charlie was finally at a real school that taught modern dance.

She hitched her bag higher on her shoulder, took a deep breath, and pushed on the heavy old door.

She could already hear music pounding from the studio above. From the thudding and clapping, it sounded like a toddler class. Or maybe junior beginners.

For months, Charlie had begged her parents to let her start dancing here. At first, they had just said no. The classes cost a lot of money. And to get here, Charlie had to catch a bus all by herself.

But two weeks ago, as a birthday surprise, Charlie's parents had said yes.

Quietly, Charlie climbed up the stairs. Soon, she came to another door and another sign.

Charlie smiled to herself. Yet another thing that was different from her old ballet classes! This dance school was the real thing.

She was still smiling as she pushed open the second door.

But as she walked in and scanned the waiting area, Charlie gulped away her smile and felt her heart pounding quickly in her chest. Suddenly, the dance school seemed a long way from home.

Grouped in a huddle in the corner were four girls about Charlie's age. They were leaning in together as they giggled and whispered. From the backpacks near the group, Charlie could tell that they all went to the same school.

But they seemed linked in other ways, too—the way they sat with their legs crossed, the cut of their T-shirts. They even wore the same funky black dance shoes.

Charlie didn't even realize she was staring. But she couldn't take her eyes off their shoes. *Oh, no!* she thought. *The shoes.*

"Can I help you?" asked one of the girls, sitting up straight and looking at Charlie.

Her hair was long and worn loose like the others. She was smiling, but her eyes seemed cold.

"Ummm," Charlie looked down at her school shoes, wondering if she should just turn around and go home. "I'm OK," she mumbled.

For some reason, she wanted to hide from the group of girls. But the waiting area was not very big.

Charlie walked a few steps to the nearest wall. She wasn't thinking straight. All she could think of was hiding.

Then another girl walked up to Charlie. She had dark, curly hair that bounced when she moved. She wasn't from the group of friends, but she wore the same black dance shoes.

"Are you looking for the bathroom?" she said. She raised her eyebrows and gave Charlie a broad smile. "It's through there."

The next thing she knew, Charlie was turning the lock in a bathroom stall. Did she say thanks to that girl? She had wanted to. But she had felt too shy to talk.

Charlie leaned against the stall door and took a gulp of air.

Never mind. Charlie couldn't worry about saying thanks now. She had other things to worry about.

Charlie unzipped her bag and looked inside. For the past four years, she had worn the same clothes to dance class—a plain black leotard, pink tights, and pink ballet shoes. Yuk.

Why was Miss Plum so old-fashioned?

Charlie was so used to the old uniform that she hadn't thought of getting new clothes for this class.

Oh, no! My clothes are so old-fashioned.

But she couldn't wear ballet shoes at a modern dance class. Could she?

Charlie shook her head and sighed. If she didn't wear her ballet shoes, what could she do? Her tights had feet in them. It would be too slippery to dance like that.

But if she didn't wear tights, what was she left with? Just a black leotard and bare legs. For some reason, that almost felt like dancing naked.

Charlie shook her head again and groaned. *How could this be happening?*

Not now!

Then she heard the thud and bang of the beginners coming out of the dance studio.

Charlie's first class in modern dance was about to start.

CHAPTER TWO

"Scissors? What do you want scissors for?"

The receptionist frowned over the counter at Charlie. She had long hair, worn loose, like everyone else.

"I . . . um . . . " Charlie didn't know what to say. She couldn't tell the receptionist what she was planning.

"You're the new girl, aren't you?" the receptionist said. But she wasn't smiling.

Charlie nodded. She could hear whispering and giggles as the girls walked behind her and into the studio.

"Make sure you bring them back," the receptionist said. Then her voice softened. "OK?"

"OK, thanks."

Charlie took the scissors and rushed back into the bathroom.

She had to work fast.

As she snipped, she thought about what her mom was going to say. But Charlie couldn't worry about that now.

Making Mom mad was better than wearing ballet shoes to a modern dance class. There was no way Charlie was going

to do that. Not in front of those trendy girls. She just couldn't!

As she stepped into her leotard, Charlie thought about taking her hair out of its ponytail and pulling off her headband. But she didn't have time to fuss with her hair. She was already late for class.

Charlie put everything except the scissors back in her bag.

She took a deep breath. This was it.

Time to face the music.

"Weeeeeeeelcome, Charlie!" Rosie, the dance teacher, yelled above the music. As she clapped her hands, her nail polish glittered. "Just find a spot at the barre."

The rest of the class stopped kicking and stared at Charlie.

Charlie could feel all eyes on her, looking at her ponytail and her plain black leotard. Under that, she wore pink tights, cut off at the knees, and below that, bare feet. She felt her cheeks burning as she clutched the barre. She wished she could disappear. It was like being naked in front of a mob of cameras.

"OK, warm up, girls."

Rosie changed the music and started counting in time.

The rest of the class stopped staring, and started kicking and stretching at the barre.

"Just copy the others, Charlie," Rosie called. "You'll be fine!"

And for most of the class, Charlie *was* fine.

Once everyone started working and stretching together, Charlie stopped feeling quite so different.

She was surprised how similar this warm-up was to her old ballet warm-up. The kicks and stretches weren't too hard at all.

The leaps across the floor were fine, too. It was pretty much the same as ballet, except the rhythm was different. When the other girls leaped across the floor, they reminded Charlie of deer—leaping with strength and power.

But when it was Charlie's turn, she felt

light and pale. She didn't know how to stop leaping like a ballet dancer.

The girl who had shown Charlie the bathroom was easily the best dancer. Her name was Kathy, and she had a dynamic, punchy way of moving. She was balanced on the floor, but she seemed to fly through each leap.

Charlie couldn't stop watching her.

Kathy is an amazing dancer!

The way Kathy moved was exactly why Charlie wanted to learn modern dance.

But then it came time to dance in the middle of the floor.

As soon as they started a dance sequence, Charlie realized that modern dance was very different from ballet.

Everything was so fast. The other girls seemed to explode out of themselves, kicking, spinning, ducking. They all had a special way of flicking their heads to the side with a rush of long hair.

Charlie fumbled and faked it for a while.

Then she just stood at the back of the room, wondering how on earth she could ever dance like that.

"Don't worry, Charlie," Rosie called out. "We've been practicing this for weeks."

Some of the girls turned and sniggered.

But Kathy didn't. She moved in front of Charlie and slowly went through the moves. Charlie smiled a thanks, and tried to copy Kathy.

But it was no use. Charlie just couldn't get into the flow. She felt so out of place —she didn't belong here at all.

Charlie had not expected modern dance to be easy, but she also hadn't expected to feel like this—so very new and so utterly, completely different.

CHAPTER THREE

"Charlotte Anderson, what on *earth*?"

Charlie's mom stood in the doorway of her bedroom, frowning. She held up Charlie's ballet tights with the feet cut out.

"Oh . . . yeah . . ." Charlie jumped up from her bed, letting the magazine she was reading drop to the floor. "I *had* to cut the feet out." Charlie cleared her throat. "I couldn't wear my ballet shoes."

"Hmmm," said Charlie's mom, shaking her head. But she didn't seem too angry. "Imagine what Miss Plum would say if she saw these tights!" Her eyes twinkled.

Charlie giggled. Now was the time to ask her mom something.

"Mom—"

Just then, Charlie's brother yelled out from his bedroom. "Moooooomm, where's my *soccer jersey?*"

Charlie's mom yelled right back at him. "It's in the *dryer*, Harry."

"Awwww, Mom!" Harry's voice came back.

There was always a lot of yelling at Charlie's house. Not because anyone was angry. That was just how everyone talked to each other.

But not Charlie. She preferred to stay quiet, or to speak face-to-face.

It was the same at school. Charlie didn't say much there, either. The only person she really talked to was her best friend, Laura. Laura wanted to be a singer and she understood Charlie better than anyone.

Now Charlie tried to make her voice loud for once. "Mom, I need new dance shoes."

"Oh, Charlotte," her mom said, shaking her head.

"All the girls wear them," Charlie said. "Pleeeeease, Mom?"

Her mom leaned down and put her hands on Charlie's shoulders. "Charlotte, you just started," she said.

Charlie nodded.

"So let's make sure you like the new classes first, OK?"

Pleeeeease, Mom!

Charlie sighed. Of course she liked them. It was just all so different from what she had imagined, that's all.

"My little butterfly!" Charlie's mom winked. "Maybe ballet suits you better, after all." She kissed Charlie on the forehead and walked out of the room.

Charlie slumped back on her bed.

A butterfly.

Her mom always called her that.

But Charlie didn't want to be a butterfly. She wanted to be able to dance strong and fast, like the rest of the class.

At the start of the next class, Charlie was feeling good. She told herself not to worry about the shoes. And this time, she didn't feel quite so out of place.

She was wearing new dancing tights that she had bought with her allowance. They were black and cut off above the knees. Over those, Charlie wore her swimsuit from last summer. It was a trendy lime green—perfect, except the straps were a bit thin.

Over the top, she wore an old black T-shirt—cut to look like a dance top, of course!

Charlie was getting pretty handy with a pair of scissors.

At the start of the class, Kathy called Charlie over to a spot at the barre. They stretched together while Kathy talked

about her gymnastics team. It sounded like a lot of work. No wonder Kathy's dancing was so good.

"Gymnastics is really hard," Kathy said, from upside down in a stretch. She looked up and smiled at Charlie. "It's not as much fun as dancing."

"OK, girls!" Rosie called out. "We need to talk about the recital."

"Yay!" Kathy whispered.

Charlie raised her eyebrows. She hadn't expected a recital!

Everyone stretched quietly while Rosie talked. The recital was only two months away, and Rosie wanted to spend more time practicing.

When Rosie said that, the trendy girls started whispering together. Even Kathy looked excited.

Then Rosie walked over to Charlie at the barre. She leaned in close enough for Charlie to see her sparkling orange nails.

"It's a little late to fit you into our dance, Charlie," Rosie said.

Charlie pulled out of her stretch and nodded shyly. She used to love her old ballet recitals. But she couldn't imagine doing a modern dance onstage!

"But I still want you to be an understudy," Rosie said, smiling. "If someone gets sick, then you dance in their place, OK?"

"Ummm . . ." Charlie wasn't sure about that. *What if someone did get sick?*

"Just watch for the first run-through," Rosie called back, as she walked over to the CD player. "Then you can copy the others!"

Kathy winked at Charlie. "Don't worry, I'll help you," she said.

Charlie just gulped.

CHAPTER FOUR

"Places, everyone!" cried Rosie.

It was time to practice the dance for the recital. But Charlie was still at the barre, stunned that she was now an understudy.

Please, don't let anyone get sick, she thought.

The rest of the class formed an excited line at the back of the room. Charlie slipped quietly around to watch from the front.

Then the music started—loud and strong, with a pulsing beat.

Boom, boom, boom.

With the beat of the music, the line of dancers started moving jerkily like a machine. Their legs were stiff. Their arms moved like cogs in a machine.

Thud, thud, clunk.

Charlie sat down and hugged her knees. The dancers were so clever. They looked just like robots!

Soon, the music changed. The clunking sounds stopped and a sweet voice started singing.

Friday night and the lights are low . . .

Now, one of the dancers broke away

from the machine. It was Kathy. She danced in the center of the room, with the other dancers still clunking like robots behind her.

Her body seemed to move exactly how the singer sounded—groovy and happy.

This dance is fantastic!

Now Charlie recognized the music. It was called "Dancing Queen," and it was the same music from the last class.

As the music quickened, Kathy's dancing got faster and more dynamic until she was leaping across the room with joy. She even started doing gymnastic flips.

Next, Kathy ran to the dancing machine, pulling the other girls' arms, and urging the robots to dance.

One by one, each of the girls broke away from the machine until, finally, the whole class was dancing together, funky and free.

You are the Dancing Queen . . .

It was the same dance sequence that Charlie had faked her way through last week. But it made sense now. Of course it was fast—it had to be. That was part of the story.

As soon as the dance finished, Rosie asked them all to start again.

This time, Charlie moved to the side of the room and copied the others. As they danced, Rosie called out instructions to the class.

"Robots, eyes on the floor."

"Shoulders down, Kathy. Good!"

"Smile, girls! You're supposed to be happy now."

By the end of the class, Charlie was buzzing. She had only managed to pick up some of the dance. But that didn't matter.

She was determined to learn the dance the right way.

The dance for the recital was fabulous!

But as Charlie pulled on her clothes in the waiting area after class, one of the trendy girls called out to her.

"What are you up to now, Charlie?"

"Oh, um . . ." Charlie looked down at her feet. *Was the girl being nice to her?*

"Looks like you're going swimming!" the girl said in a nasty voice.

One of her friends laughed. Another friend hit the first girl on the arm.

Charlie felt blood rushing to her cheeks and a lump form in her throat. She wanted to run away and hide again.

"I like your bathing suit, Charlie," Kathy said, pulling on a sweater and smiling. Her curly hair bounced on her shoulders. "That color is cool!"

"Yeah, don't worry about me, Charlie," said the trendy girl. "I was only teasing."

She said it like it was a good thing. Then she made a hissing noise and scratched her hand in the air like a cat.

The others did the same, and laughed.

They seemed to have forgotten about Charlie and Kathy.

Kathy rolled her big eyes. "I'll walk you downstairs," she said.

Charlie walked with Kathy in silence down the stairs. The shrieks and laughter of the trendy girls filtered down to them.

When Charlie said bye to Kathy, she tried to smile, but she didn't really feel like it. Kathy was nice. But Charlie didn't like the other girls.

Being new wasn't just about dancing, it was about fitting in. But nothing Charlie did seemed good enough for the trendy girls.

CHAPTER FIVE

"You are the Dancing Queen," Laura's voice sang out among the trees as Charlie practiced the dance at school.

There was a spot, right behind the pine tree area, that was almost hidden from view. It was the only place where Charlie didn't feel too shy to dance at school.

Sometimes, someone would run past

playing tag, but usually the other kids didn't go near them.

As Charlie danced, the dry pine needles kicked up around her feet.

Kick and lean back . . . swivel on two feet . . .

Charlie was getting used to the speed of the dance now. She had been practicing for weeks. At night, she would pull open the curtains in the living room, and use the windows as mirrors.

She must have done the dance a hundred times by now!

In fact, she had practiced so many times that it didn't even feel fast anymore. The dance just felt happy and free.

Sometimes, Charlie even felt like she

had time within the dance to reach out a little further or to kick a little higher.

Time, even, to dream that *she* was the Dancing Queen.

As Laura hummed the end of the song, Charlie leapt to the side of her pretend stage for the end of the dance.

"Yay, Charlie!" Laura clapped. "You make it look easy."

Charlie smiled and shrugged.

The dancing was easier now. In fact, her old ballet training had come in handy. But she still didn't feel like she fit in at the new dance school.

"Bet you're the best in the class," Laura said.

Charlie let out a small laugh and shook her head.

Then Laura started singing again.

"Charlie's the Dancing Queen, shy and sweet, see her tiny feet!"

They both laughed and sat down on the roots of a tall pine tree.

"I'll never be the best in the class," Charlie said after a while.

"Yeah, right!" Laura started pushing pine needles into a big pile.

"I'm not . . ." Charlie searched for the right words. "I'm too . . . *different*."

Laura shifted over so that she was sitting on her pile of pine needles like it was a cushion.

"That's just because you're new," Laura said. She started pushing more pine needles into a new pile.

Charlie shrugged. She wasn't so new anymore. The trendy girls didn't tease Charlie now, not like that time with the swimsuit. But they still weren't very nice to her, either.

They never said hello or bye to Charlie. They were always too busy giggling and whispering in a group.

When Charlie finally came to class wearing real dance shoes, the trendy girls didn't even notice!

She didn't have any idea how to make them like her. She still didn't know how to fit in.

But after weeks of classes at the new dance school, Charlie did know one thing.

She knew that she loved to dance.

"Your throne, my lady," Laura said in a posh voice. She pointed at a new pile of pine needles.

Charlie giggled.

Then she sat on her throne, laughing and pretending to be a queen.

CHAPTER SIX

Charlie sat under the barre and hugged her knees.

The new costumes glittered and shimmered as the rest of the class held them up with *oooh*s and *aaah*s.

Charlie sighed quietly. There was no costume for Charlie. She wasn't in the recital, so she didn't need one.

"Put it around your neck like this,"

Rosie said, showing the class how to put on their costumes.

As Charlie watched, the rest of the class tried their costumes on. They looked like shiny metal robots.

Charlie sighed again.

When she had first heard about the recital, she had been scared stiff. But that felt like a long time ago. Now that she knew the dance so well, Charlie thought she could dance onstage if she had to.

In fact, maybe wearing the costume and dancing onstage would be fun.

"When you break away from the machine," Rosie said, "you do this." She pulled at the Velcro on Kathy's costume.

As the silver material came away, Rosie pulled it in a glittering circle. Then she wrapped it around Kathy's waist to make a shimmery skirt.

It glittered and rippled over Kathy's hips as she moved.

"Ooooooh!" said everyone.

The rest of the class copied. Soon, they were all standing together in sparkling dancing skirts.

Charlie rested her chin on her knees. She wanted to reach out and touch the shiny skirts.

"OK, OK!" Rosie clapped her hands. "Costumes off while we warm up."

"Awww!" the girls groaned.

"You can put them back on after that," Rosie said, smiling.

When it happened, Charlie was in another world.

In her mind, she was a clunking robot, stuck in a machine and forced to do the same work day after day.

It didn't matter that she was dancing to the side, away from the rest of the class. It didn't even matter that she wasn't wearing a costume.

In her mind, Charlie was a robot, about to break away from the machine and be free. When Kathy broke away, Charlie kept jolting and jerking like the others.

That was when it happened.

Kathy was smiling, broad and big as always. She pulled the costume from around her neck and wrapped it around her waist. She twirled and leapt with the skirt flowing around her.

Then Kathy jumped back into one flip, and then another. . . .

But this time, as Kathy flipped back, the new skirt got caught under her hands. As Kathy pushed off, her hands slipped on the skirt.

With a cry, Kathy crashed awkwardly to the floor.

It took Charlie a while to come out of her daydream and realize what had happened. But when she did, she felt sick watching.

Kathy was groaning and sobbing while Rosie put an ice pack on her ankle.

Before long, Rosie had carried Kathy out into the waiting area.

Soon, everyone heard the receptionist talking on the phone to Kathy's mom.

". . . You should probably take Kathy to the hospital."

Charlie gulped and shook her head.

Not Kathy.

And not now! It was only three weeks until the recital.

The trendy girls were whispering in a group. But they seemed more excited than worried.

Charlie glanced at the rest of the class. Then she tiptoed to the waiting area and peeked around the door.

Kathy was lying on the floor with her ankle propped up on a chair. Her cheeks and hair were wet with tears. Rosie and the receptionist were talking quickly in another room.

Poor Kathy! Charlie knelt on the floor beside her friend.

"Oh Kathy, don't cry," Charlie whispered. "It'll be all right."

Kathy took a quivering breath. "I'm going to miss the recital. . . ."

Charlie shook her head. But she knew Kathy was right.

". . . *and* level tests at gymnastics!" Kathy continued.

Then she started crying again.

Charlie held her friend's hand, wishing she knew what to say.

After a while, Kathy took a big gulp of air.

"At least you'll have a spot in the dance," Kathy said, trying to smile. "That's one good thing."

Charlie shook her head again. She still didn't know what to say.

Being in the recital and wearing the costume would be wonderful. But she didn't want Kathy to miss out.

Right now, Charlie didn't know what to hope for.

CHAPTER *SEVEN*

When Kathy had left for the hospital, Rosie walked back into the studio, frowning.

The whole class watched as she walked to the CD player and tapped her fingernails on the lid.

Rat-a-tat-tat. Rat-a-tat-tat.

Everyone was quiet, watching.

"Well!" Rosie tried to smile, but her eyes looked worried. "Change of plans."

Charlie held her breath.

Rosie walked around from behind the CD player and stood in front of the class.

She looked at Charlie.

"Lucky we have an understudy," Rosie said.

Charlie nodded but she didn't smile. It all seemed so serious. And something else was worrying her.

Right away one of the trendy girls said out loud what was worrying Charlie.

"But what about Kathy's solo?"

The whole class looked up at Rosie. *What about Kathy's solo?*

"Well, there's not much time, but we'll have to hold an audition." Rosie scanned the girls in the class. "I want you all to try out for the part of the Dancing Queen."

Until now, everyone had been quiet. But suddenly everyone—everyone except Charlie—started talking at once.

"But how can we?"

"Kathy's solo has all those flippy things in it!"

I can't replace Kathy.

"We can't do that!"

Rosie yelled above the noise and clapped her hands in a glitter of nail polish.

"OK, OK!" Rosie yelled.

When the room was quiet, she continued talking.

"Now, girls. Our dance isn't about flips." Rosie put her hands on her hips. "Can anyone tell me what our dance *is* about?"

Everyone was quiet.

"Being happy?" someone said, after a while.

"Dancing with your friends?" said someone else.

Charlie hugged her knees and looked at her dancing shoes. She loved the dance.

For her, doing the dance was like living a perfect dream.

"Well, for me," said Rosie, "the dance is about being yourself. The Dancing Queen breaks away from the crowd and dances her own special dance."

Rosie smiled at the class.

"Next week, I want you all to show me your own special dance. Whatever that is. It doesn't have to have flips."

Rosie smiled at Charlie. "You, too, Charlie," Rosie said. "I want *everyone* to try out. Show me the dance that comes from your heart."

When Rosie said that, everyone started talking again.

Charlie kept hugging her knees, but she couldn't help smiling. In just one class, everything had changed so much. Now she didn't just have a spot in the dance, she was also allowed to try out for the main part!

After class that night, Charlie pulled open the curtains in the living room so she could see herself in the windows.

Her mom's voice floated in from the kitchen. "You are the Daaancing Queeeen . . ."

Charlie's mom wasn't a very good singer. She sounded like an opera singer with a sore throat. But it was nice of her to be excited for Charlie.

When Charlie had told her mom that she was going to be in the recital, Charlie's mom had given her a bear hug.

"Lucky we bought those dancing shoes!" she had said.

But now Charlie had more than dancing shoes to worry about.

Keeping an eye on her reflection in the window, Charlie danced through Kathy's solo. She had watched Kathy do it so many times that she already knew it by heart.

In the parts where Kathy did her gymnastic flips, Charlie worked out some leaps and turns to do instead. But she still felt like a butterfly, just like her mom had said.

She could tell she wasn't half as good as Kathy. The punchy, bold parts looked so good when Kathy did them. But Charlie didn't feel at all like a queen when she tried to copy. She felt weak and silly.

Charlie flopped down on the carpet and made a face at the window.

What was the point? Rosie would never pick Charlie to be the Dancing Queen. She was the newest in the class, after all.

But until Rosie picked someone else next week, Charlie could dream.

CHAPTER EIGHT

"When is it? I'll have to come!"

At school the next day, Laura gave Charlie a hug. She seemed even more excited about the recital than Charlie.

"But there's more," Charlie said over Laura's shoulder.

Laura pulled away from the hug to look at her. "More?"

"Kathy was the Dancing Queen. . . ."

Charlie trailed off. *Poor Kathy.* She must be so disappointed. "So we all get to try out for her part."

"Oooooo!" Laura's eyes were wide. "They'll pick you for sure!"

Charlie laughed and shook her head. "I knew you would say that, Laura!"

"Well, it's true," Laura said, grinning. "You keep saying how differently you dance."

The bell rang and they both picked up their bags.

"That's what the dance is about, isn't it?" Laura said. "Being different?"

Charlie just shrugged.

But for the rest of the day, she kept thinking about the part of the Dancing

Queen. Laura's words had given Charlie
an idea.

Maybe being different wasn't so bad
after all.

After school, Charlie was back in the
living room at home. She put "Dancing
Queen" on the CD player and pressed
repeat.

Then she stood in the center of the
room, listening and swaying to the music.

But this time, Charlie didn't worry
about Kathy's solo or her gymnastic flips.
She didn't worry about trying to fit in.

She didn't even worry about what she looked like in the window.

Charlie listened to the sweet voice and shut her eyes. She let the tune and rhythm settle inside.

As she swayed to the music, Charlie thought about everything that had happened to her.

Begging her parents to let her start at the new dance school.

Hiding from the trendy girls on her first day.

Trying to dance like the others and feeling weak, like a butterfly.

Charlie let it all flow through her— feeling so different, learning so much and now loving how the dance made her feel.

Then Charlie started to dance.

As she moved, all her feelings seemed to flow out through her body.

It was like the words hiding inside were now coming out as she danced. Reaching to the side felt like it was for hope and yearning. Charlie pulled in for sadness, and hid safe in her own arms.

Then she leapt in joy.

The soft flow of an arm movement felt like a peaceful dream. Charlie leaned back, feeling shy, and then exploded out, just because she was alive.

Slowly, section by section, Charlie felt her way through her new dance. Each time she went through it, she relived everything through her body. It was like dancing in her own, private world.

When she was finished, Charlie felt

clear and calm. She felt happy.

And feeling the way she did, Charlie stopped worrying about being picked to be the Dancing Queen. Right now, she felt too good to worry about that.

The story of the Dancing Queen became Charlie's story about being different, and fitting in. After being so shy and scared, Charlie felt like she had finally found her voice.

CHAPTER NINE

For the rest of the week, Charlie felt calm.
Even when she wasn't practicing her
dance, she still felt different, like she was
holding a smile in her heart.

Whenever she had a chance, Charlie
practiced her solo—changing moves here
and adding an extra flourish there.

She even tried leaving her hair loose
and flipping it around like the rest of the

class. But in the end, Charlie tied her hair back into a ponytail. It felt better that way.

Over the weekend, Charlie called her mom into the living room to show her the new dance.

At first, Charlie's mom kept flipping through her address book, only half watching Charlie.

But as Charlie kept dancing, her mom put the address book down. Soon a funny, surprised look came over her mom's face.

When Charlie finished her solo, her mom was quiet, staring at Charlie with the same surprised look on her face.

"What's wrong, Mom?" asked Charlie. "Don't you like it?"

"Oh, Charlotte," her mom shook her head in wonder. "It's beautiful."

At school, Laura started calling Charlie the Dancing Queen, and told everyone about the audition. When the teacher wished Charlie luck, everyone stared at her. But she held the calm feeling in her heart and didn't feel like blushing at all.

Charlie felt happy right until the next dance class—the audition.

As she walked up the stairs to the dance school, she even felt excited about showing everyone her solo. Maybe Rosie would like Charlie's dance as much as her mom did.

But then, as she opened the door, Charlie saw the trendy girls. They were wearing their costumes, and had ultra-stylish hair. One of them was even wearing makeup.

The other girls look so stylish.

As Charlie walked past them, she felt the calmness trickle away and disappear, like it was hiding out of reach. With that came the rush of worries—wondering what the trendy girls would think, and fretting that she didn't have a costume.

She wondered why she had bothered to come today at all. Rosie would never pick her for the main part!

All through the auditions, Charlie sat in a corner, hugging her knees.

She could tell that the trendy girls had been practicing together. Their solos were a lot like Kathy's. And in the parts they had changed, all four did the same head flips and hip rocks.

Finally, everyone except Charlie had had her turn.

"OK Charlie, best for last!" Rosie called.

Charlie stood up and ducked under the barre. As she walked to the center of the room, her heart pounded in her chest——

stronger than ever before. She felt all eyes on her——no costume, her cheeks red.

Silly Charlie.

The music started and the sweet voice began to sing.

Friday night and the lights are low . . .

But Charlie couldn't move. It felt like the voice was singing for someone else, someone like the trendy girls. It didn't feel like the song was for Charlie anymore.

Charlie shut her eyes and tried to hold the voice inside like before. But all she could feel was the thudding of her heart.

Suddenly, the music stopped.

"What's wrong, Charlie?" Rosie asked kindly.

Charlie shook her head.

She could hardly breathe, let alone talk.

"I . . . I *can't*," Charlie said.

One of the trendy girls whispered something to the others.

Charlie shook her head again. "I don't want to. . . ."

I can't do it!

But she felt like crying when she heard her own words.

Rosie was quiet for a while, tapping the lid of the CD player.

Then she nodded.

"OK, girls. I'll give you the answer next week," she said.

In a fog, Charlie went and sat with the rest of the class. She wished she were someone else, like the trendy girls— always happy and never scared.

Life would be so much better that way.

CHAPTER TEN

At the end of the class, Rosie called Charlie over to talk.

"Kathy's mom is going to drop by with her costume this week," Rosie said.

Charlie nodded down at her shoes. She hated herself for being so shy.

"How is Kathy?" Charlie asked quietly.

"She's OK, poor thing," Rosie said. "She's coming to watch the recital."

Charlie managed to look up at Rosie and smile.

But Rosie looked thoughtful. "Why don't you show me your solo now?" she said. "I'd love to see it."

"Oh," Charlie glanced out the door to the waiting area. She could hear the rest of the class talking and laughing together.

"Hang on." Rosie ran over and shut the door. Then she gently led Charlie by the shoulders to the center of the room. "Just dance for me," Rosie said. "OK?"

Charlie wanted to shake her head. Then the music started.

Friday night and the lights are low . . .

Somehow, with the other girls out of

the room, Charlie felt the sweet voice reaching inside her like before.

Before she could think, Charlie was dancing. But not just dancing—she was feeling it all inside, coming from her heart. The hope and fear and joy all came out as Charlie danced for her teacher just like when she danced at home.

When Charlie had finished, Rosie smiled and nodded.

"See you next week," she said.

Everyone was stunned.

The whole class stared at Rosie with

mouths open and eyes wide.

It was the week after the audition, less than one week until the recital.

Charlie couldn't see her own face, but she knew that she must have looked more stunned than anyone.

What did Rosie just say?

"Me?" she stammered. "I—"

Her heart was pounding again, but not like last week. Part of her felt good. She was surprised and scared, but also happy. *Thrilled.*

"I know you had a case of stage fright last week," Rosie said. "But I'm sure you can do it, Charlie."

The trendy girls were whispering to each other as they looked at Charlie.

Charlie shook her head. "I can't," she said. *Not with everyone watching,* she thought.

"Here," Rosie said kindly. She gave Charlie a bag. "Just put on Kathy's costume and give it a go."

Charlie nodded and ran to the bathroom. She was glad to escape from the eyes of the rest of the class.

Once she was safely inside the bath-

room stall, Charlie put her hand over her mouth and laughed out loud.

She couldn't believe it! Rosie had asked her to be the Dancing Queen!

She couldn't imagine doing her dance in front of the trendy girls, and definitely not at the recital!

But it still felt great to be asked.

Charlie pulled the shimmery costume out of the bag and carefully pulled it on.

It felt fantastic.

She leaned back, all glittery, against the door. Then she took a long, deep breath.

Rosie must have thought Charlie's solo was good. But was it good enough to dance in the recital?

What if she had stage fright again?

Charlie took another breath and shook her head. No, she was too shy to dance her solo for the recital. She would have to tell Rosie to choose someone else.

Charlie picked up the empty bag, ready to go back and talk to Rosie.

But then she stopped.

The bag wasn't empty.

At the bottom of the bag was a small package with Charlie's name on it.

Inside was a delicate plastic butterfly. Its wings were white and shimmery.

She peered at the delicate wings, smiling. They reminded her of something. . . .

Then she noticed a note tucked into the wrapping.

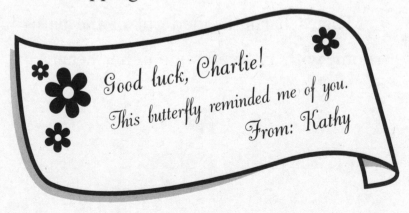

Good luck, Charlie!
This butterfly reminded me of you.
From: Kathy

Charlie smiled at the note. Kathy was so kind. Right from the start, she had been nice to Charlie. She didn't care that Charlie was different.

Why then, did Charlie worry about the trendy girls? It didn't matter what they thought. Charlie already had a friend in the class. A *good* friend. After a while, she tucked the butterfly and note safely back in the bag.

Then Charlie headed out of the bathroom, with a secret smile in her heart.

CHAPTER ELEVEN

It was very dark. Charlie heard a cough from the audience, then the shuffling of feet as she and her class ran onto the stage.

Together, they formed a human machine. Arms linked, bodies close, all of them waiting as one.

Charlie could feel the familiar pounding in her chest. But she could also feel something else inside—another feeling that she knew quite well.

Then the music started, pounding through the theater.

Boom, boom, boom.

With it came the flashing strobe light and the clunking of the machine.

Charlie jerked her arms in time with the others. Right now, she looked like them, and moved like them. She could even sense that she felt like them.

But she wasn't exactly the same.

As the music kept thudding, Charlie could feel her class tensing around her. They all knew what came next.

For a moment, Charlie's mind went blank and time seemed to stand still.

Then the flashing light stopped and the music changed. The whole theater seemed to hold its breath.

As the sweet voice rang out, Charlie felt it touch her inside.

Friday night and the lights are low . . .

With all eyes on her, Charlie pulled the costume from around her neck and wrapped it around her waist.

Then she was dancing. She twirled and leaped, kicked and reached.

Charlie still couldn't see the audience, but she knew they were all there—Kathy, Laura, her family. Even Miss Plum was there. They had all come to see Charlie dance.

But she wasn't just dancing for them. She was also dancing because she loved it. She felt like a butterfly flitting in the sunlight and, right now, that felt wonderful.

As the lights shone stronger, Charlie moved to the machine. She pulled at the

girls' arms, urging them to break away and be free. From the looks on their faces, Charlie could understand how the other girls felt—funky and fabulous.

Soon, the whole class was dancing together in the middle of the stage.

Then, too soon, it came time to leap offstage for the ending.

In an instant, the theater roared to life with claps and cheers. Charlie even heard a whooping sound from her brother.

But the class was in another world.

Together, they ran out of the wings, giggling and shushing each other in the corridor and then laughing and hugging in the dressing room.

Charlie even hugged the trendy girls.

"Charlie, how did you do it?" one of them asked. "I would have been scared stiff."

Charlie laughed. "I *was* scared stiff!"

Then they hugged and laughed again.

After the recital, Charlie and her class changed back into their normal clothes again. Everyone was still flushed with excitement. Plus, they only had a short break until the start of the next recital, when they would have to dance all over again.

"We're heading to the café for some food," one of the trendy girls called out.

"Who wants to come?"

Some of the other girls picked up their purses and headed for the door.

Charlie managed to look the trendy girl in the eye. "No thanks, Holly."

It felt good calling her by name.

She was, after all, a normal person.

"Maybe next time?" Charlie asked.

"OK," Holly nodded and smiled. Then she headed out the door with the others.

Charlie sat down on the dressing room floor and looked around. It felt good to be alone. But Charlie didn't want to hide in here.

She wanted to go outside and see her family, and Laura, and to say hi to Miss Plum.

But most of all, Charlie wanted to find Kathy. She had something to give her.

Charlie pulled it carefully from the corner of her makeup bag. It was a statue of a deer in the middle of a leap. It looked graceful and powerful, exactly like Kathy.

Charlie didn't have a note for Kathy, but she hoped Kathy would understand. The right present can say a lot.

After all, two people can still be friends, even if they both dance completely different.

THE END

It's her first PJ party!
But what if something
embarrassing happens?

CHAPTER ✿ ONE

It was six o'clock on Friday morning, the last day of school for the year. The alarm hadn't gone off yet, but Olivia was already awake, dressed, and sitting at the kitchen table, eating her toast and waiting for her mom to get up.

She drank a glass of milk and ate an apple, but her mom still slept on. She brushed her teeth and made her lunch, but even then her mom did not stir.

Olivia checked the clock on the microwave. Six thirty. Surely her mom should be awake by now? She tiptoed along the hallway and looked in. Her mom was fast asleep, snoring slightly. Olivia knocked gently on the open door. Her mom did not move.

Olivia cleared her throat, "Ahem!"

Her mom rolled over in bed and snored more loudly. Olivia was getting desperate.

"Mom," she whispered.

"Mom," she said gently.

"Mom!" she said more firmly.

This was getting her nowhere.

"MOM!" she yelled suddenly and stamped her foot.

"Hmm?" said her mom, sitting up in bed, her hair all fluffy on one side. "What's up, baby?"

"Mom," said Olivia. "You have to get up. I am sleeping over at Ching Ching's house tonight."

"Are you?" said her mom. "Are you sure? Did we talk about this?"

"Mom," said Olivia sternly, because she had to be strict with her mom sometimes. "You know it is. We talked about it on Monday, remember? You spoke with Mrs. Adams on the phone."

"I know, baby," said her mom,

yawning. "I'm just teasing you."

"Well," said Olivia, "will you get up now?"

"Mmm," said her mom, still sounding tired. "What time is it?"

"Six thirty," said Olivia. "Or even later by now. We've been talking for at least five minutes."

"Six thirty?"

"Or six thirty-five," said Olivia.

"Is the sun even up yet?" asked her mom.

"Mom!"

"OK, OK," said her mom. "I'm getting up. Even though it's still the middle of the night," she grumbled.

"Come on," said Olivia. "Here's your bathrobe."

———————————————

While her mom took a shower, Olivia checked her bag again. As well as her lunchbox, she had packed her pajamas, her swimsuit, some clean clothes for tomorrow, her hairbrush, and a small box of chocolates for Ching Ching's mom, to say thank you. Was that everything?

It was almost seven o'clock and Olivia was dancing with impatience, waiting for her mom to finish blow-drying her hair. Finally, she was ready.

"OK," she said to Olivia. "Now, are you sure you have packed everything you need?"

"Yes," said Olivia.

"Pajamas?"

"Yes," said Olivia.

"Chocolates for Mrs. Adams?"

"Yes," said Olivia.

"Clean underwear for tomorrow?"

"Mom!"

"Well, have you?"

"YES!" said Olivia. "Come on!"

"All right!" said her mom. "Just checking.

I'll just get the keys. . . . "

But Olivia was already out the door and waiting at the front gate, her backpack on her back. Her mom locked the door and walked down the path (so slowly!), and together they walked to the bus stop.

"I'm going to miss you tonight," said her mom.

"Yeah, yeah," said Olivia, looking ahead for the bus.

"I will. I won't see you all day, I won't have anyone to eat dinner with, and you'll be at Ching Ching's until tomorrow. . . . "

"I know," said Olivia.

"What time am I picking you up?"

"Lunchtime," said Olivia. "Ching Ching

and I will have breakfast together, and play in the morning, and then you can pick me up at lunchtime."

"Lunchtime it is," said her mom, giving her a hug and a big smoochy kiss.

The bus was just arriving at the corner.

"Bye, mom," said Olivia, yelling back over her shoulder as she ran to catch it.

At last she was on her way.

❁

What will she do when her sister cuts off her hair?

GO GIRL!

SiSTeR
SPiRiT

BY **THALIA KALKIPSAKIS**

Keep reading for an excerpt!

CHAPTER ✿ ONE

My big sister Hannah hates me and I know why. It's because I was born after her.

When Hannah was three, I was born. Everyone said I was *sooooooo cute!* Mom says they stopped saying Hannah was cute, so she threw all my baby clothes down the toilet.

I look younger than I really am. I'm nine years old, but sometimes people think

I look six or seven.

Hannah calls me a baby doll, but she doesn't mean it in a nice way. She says I should try to look my age, but it's not my fault! I can't change how I look.

But now, it's even worse than ever. Hannah cut off my hair and Mom went crazy on her. Then Hannah stopped talking to me.

Strange, isn't it? Hannah cut off my hair and got into trouble, and she blames me for it!

She must really hate me, that girl. Let me explain.

We were watching TV and a show came on about hair. It said that a haircut can change the way you look. It can make you look older or younger.

Hannah said, "Maybe if we cut your hair, people wouldn't think you're so cute anymore!"

"Yeah," I said, not really listening.

Hannah turned off the TV. "Aren't you sick of people saying how cute you look?" she asked.

"Yeah," I said again, but now I *was* listening.

"So why don't we cut your hair short, so you look your age?" Hannah said.

I wasn't sure. It sounded exciting, cutting my hair. I liked the idea of doing something different and looking older. But it's a big

thing to cut off all your hair. And I've had
long hair all my life.

"But what would Mom say?" I said.

"Mom!" Hannah rolled her eyes. Her
hair is dark and shoulder length. It kinks
up around her ears.

"Why do you always worry what Mom

thinks? It's not Mom's hair, " she said.

She had a point. It wasn't Mom's hair, it was *my* hair.

"Come on, let's do it." Hannah's eyes looked bright with excitement.

It was exciting to do something like this together, just her and me. It felt a bit like the stories you read of sisters going shopping and trying on clothes together. It felt good—like Hannah liked me.

It also seemed a little naughty to do something without Mom knowing.

"OK," I said. "Let's do it."

Hannah smiled.

I bet my eyes looked as bright and excited as Hannah's.